For Shelley, Phoebe, Holly,
Alice and Belle,
with much appreciation for their
interesting chicken personalities

www.mascotbooks.com

# Why Didn't the Chicken Cross the Road?

Layout and Design by Paulette Webb

**For more information, please contact:**
Mascot Books
620 Herndon Parkway, Suite 320
Herndon, VA 20170
info@mascotbooks.com

Library of Congress Control Number: 2020902727

CPSIA Code: PRTWP0720A
ISBN-13: 978-1-64543-411-5

Printed in South Korea

# Why **DIDN'T** the Chicken Cross the Road?

**Written and Illustrated
by Paul Schwartz**

LEMONADE !!

"Look over there! It looks soooo nice,"
said the blue alligator.

**From across the road Chicken heard,
"Hey Chicken! Why don't you come over?"**

Mommy chicken said, "I don't
think you should cross the road.
Some chickens cross the road
and never come back."

Daddy chicken said, "I heard that flying monkeys pick them up and carry them away."

"Hey you, Chicken! We're having
popsicles for lunch!"

"I think I'm going to cross the road."

Mommy chicken said, "Did you see
how fast that car was going?
It is so dangerous to cross the road."

Daddy chicken said, "I think that car was looking for a chicken to run over."

Chicken's friends called
out from across the road,
"Hey Chicken! What
are you waiting for?
We're playing Duck
Duck Goose!"

"I really think I'm going to cross the road!"

Mommy chicken said, "Just make sure
you have clean underpants, in case
you get hurt and go to the hospital."

Daddy chicken said, "Urk! The food is terrible at the hospital!"

"Maybe I'll cross the road tomorrow."

Chicken was sad for a minute.
Then he had an idea.

"What is our little chicken doing now?"
said Daddy chicken to Mommy chicken.

"Look! I made a bridge!"

The End

"I'm afraid to cross the road, too."

# About the Author

Paul Schwartz is an environmental lawyer, folk artist, guitar player and songwriter who lives in Atlanta, Georgia, with his family. He was a member of the relatively unknown rock bands Big Fish Ensemble and Lord High Admirals, and takes care of backyard chickens. This is his first children's book.